DAUGHTERS OF DISCIPLINE

MARYAM RAHMAN

To all the girls who were silenced in the name of obedience
who still chose to fight.
And to the ones who died fighting.
You matter. Always.

Contents

Content Warning

This book contains sensitive material that may be distressing to some readers. *Daughters of Discipline* explores themes of institutional and child abuse, emotional manipulation, grief, loss, and the psychological aftermath of trauma. It includes depictions of violence, panic attacks, and systemic neglect, as well as references to suicide ideation and the death of a child. While the story ultimately centers on survival, sisterhood, and reclaiming power, it does not shy away from the darker truths its characters endure. Reader discretion is advised—please care for your heart as you read.

Preface

I didn't plan to write Daughters of Discipline. I was deep into another story when this one came knocking—loud, fierce, and impossible to ignore. What started as a detour turned into an escape. A place I could pour all the hurt, hope, and healing I didn't know I was carrying.

This book means the world to me. I hope, in some way, it finds a place in yours too.

— Maryam Rahman

Acknowledgements

Thank you to Miya and Zip—my best hype besties—for always being there, for believing in me, and for supporting every story I've poured my heart into. Love you both endlessly.

To the beta readers who offered their honest feedback while still respecting my creative choices—thank you for helping me grow as a writer without dimming my voice.

To Notion Press, for giving me the space and platform to bring this book to life.

To my parents, for everything—your support, your love, your faith in me.

And to my writer self—for holding on through doubt, deadlines, and wild plot twists. I'm proud of you.

— Maryam

Foreword

Reading Daughters of Discipline felt like stumbling into a quiet storm. It's haunting in the best way—thoughtful, raw, and unflinchingly honest. Maryam Rahman has crafted something that stays with you, long after you've turned the last page.

It's not just a book. It's a conversation that matters.

— A Beta Reader

Playlist

"Control" – Halsey
"The One That Got Away" (Acoustic) – Katy Perry
"Heavy in Your Arms" – Florence + the Machine
"Castle" – Halsey
"Youth" – Daughter
"bury a friend" – Billie Eilish
"Runaway" – AURORA
"The Archer" – Taylor Swift
"Elastic Heart" – Sia
"Bird Set Free" – Sia
"My Tears Ricochet" – Taylor Swift
"Lilith (Diablo IV Anthem)" – Halsey
"Labour" – Paris Paloma
"Celestial" – Ed Sheeran
"The End" – Phoebe Ryan
"Secret for the Mad" – dodie
"Youth" – Shawn Mendes & Khalid
"Flowers" – Lauren Spencer Smith

About Author

Maryam Rahman has always believed in the power of stories—especially the ones that burn, bruise, and bloom all at once. *Daughters of Discipline* is her boldest step yet into the world of storytelling, where pain and resilience dance hand in hand. While she's always had a soft spot for romantic comedies, this book was something else entirely—a story that demanded to be written. A story for the silenced, the shattered, and the survivors. Though her roots lie in love stories, Maryam is endlessly curious and eager to explore as many genres and narrative styles as she finds meaningful. To her, reading and writing are escapes into worlds that never truly die, places where truth wears many faces and healing begins with a single word. This book is dedicated to those who have been hurt—and those who chose to rise anyway.

Prologue

The road twisted like a serpent in prayer, flanked by trees that grew too straight to be trusted. No birds sang above them—only the occasional rustle, as if the forest itself was holding its breath. In the backseat of the car, Mara sat with her knees pressed tightly together, hands clenched into fists on her lap. Her fingernails had dug crescent marks into her skin several bends ago, but she made no move to loosen them. The pain kept her present. Anchored.

Unapologetically alive.

Leah sat beside her, humming. Not a song, not a tune—just a low, wordless sound that buzzed like a mosquito in a jar. Her way of fending off the silence, of pretending the air wasn't thick with things left unsaid. Leah's mother hadn't even come. No goodbye, no warning. Mara was all she had, and they both knew it.

The adults in the front said nothing. Mara's mother stared straight ahead, her hands white-knuckling the steering wheel like it was the only thing keeping her from crumbling. Her father hadn't spoken since they'd passed the city limits. When Mara had asked too many questions in class, when she'd dared to stand up and challenge Mr. Rourke's lecture on "moral womanhood," he hadn't yelled. He'd simply folded the newspaper, looked over his glasses, and said, *There's a place that helps girls like you find their quiet.* And that was the end of the conversation.

They pulled into the driveway of a place that didn't look like a punishment at all. The building stood three stories tall, whitewashed and windowed, surrounded by hedges trimmed into perfect, unnatural symmetry. The flowerbeds were pristine. The steps were polished. The air smelled like rosewater and cedarwood and something vaguely medicinal. It was too perfect. The kind of perfect that hurt your teeth.

There were no security cameras, no barbed wire, no signs with capital-letter rules. No warnings. No threats. Just cleanliness so clinical it felt invasive.

Leah touched Mara's hand, tentative and hopeful. "It's... nice, right?" she asked.

Mara didn't answer. Her eyes were on the windows. Each one gleamed like a mirror—but none of them reflected anything back.

Inside, the walls swallowed sound. Footsteps vanished mid-step. The hallways stretched too long, too straight, too silent. Portraits of women lined the corridors, all dressed in modest tones, their painted smiles identical and wide. Not a single speck of dust marked the frames.

They were led to the Warden's office, though no one used the word *warden*. The plaque on the door read *Administrator Annora*. The door itself was tall, painted bone-white, with a wooden cross hung precisely one inch too far to the left. Mara noticed. She always noticed.

The door opened before anyone knocked. A woman stood there—not tall, not young, but exact in every movement. Her face was powdered and pale, her mouth shaped in a smile that looked like it had been worn too often. Her eyes were gray and cold, like a sky about to thunder but refusing to rain.

"You must be Mara," she said. Her voice was soft. Too soft. As if she measured every decibel. "And you've brought a sister. How lovely. Girls are stronger in pairs... until one learns faster than the other."

Leah offered a hesitant smile. Mara remained still, spine rigid, eyes fixed on the woman like she was trying to decide if they were prey or threat.

The woman stepped aside, gesturing them in. "Come. You'll like it here. We encourage grace. Reflection. Silence. There's nothing cruel in quiet. Only healing."

Mara didn't move at first. There was something about the space beyond the threshold, the way the room didn't echo, the way her skin itched without touch. But Leah stepped forward, so Mara did too. The door clicked shut behind them—not loud, but final.

"We don't scream here," the woman said, her smile lingering as she folded her hands like a prayer. "We sing."

Mara said nothing. But somewhere deep in her chest, something old and feral stirred awake.

CHAPTER I

They painted my mouth with sugar and said,
"Sweet girls never rot."

But I tasted blood in the frosting.Mara woke to the scent of lavender—artificial, clingy, too heavy in the lungs. For a moment she thought she was home, and that none of this had happened. That she'd never climbed those polished stairs. That the cross hadn't hung one inch off-center. But the ceiling above her wasn't cracked plaster and glow-in-the-dark stars. It was spotless white, too white, with corners so precise they felt weaponized.

Her bed was one of six in the room, each one identical, tucked under thin wool blankets in shades of pale blue. Leah was already up, perched at the edge of her own bed, arms wrapped around her knees like she could hold herself together that way. Her eyes flicked to Mara the second she stirred.

"They ring a bell when it's time to wash," Leah whispered, like the silence had rules.

Mara sat up slowly. The floor was cold. The air colder. She glanced toward the window—bars, decorative maybe, but bars all the same. Her body knew before her mind could catch up: this place was not a home. It was a system wrapped in soft linens and polite smiles.

The bell rang then, exactly as Leah had said. It wasn't harsh or shrill—just one soft chime, melodic and brief. The kind of sound you might expect in a cathedral before a prayer. But it made Mara's skin crawl.

The other girls moved with practiced ease, rising without words. No one spoke. They walked in a line toward the washroom, toothbrushes already in hand. One girl turned her head slightly toward Mara as she passed—her gaze flickering, quick and unreadable—but didn't pause.

Mara stepped down and followed, because that's what one did here. Fall in line. Obey the bell.

The washroom was filled with mirrors, yet somehow it reflected nothing true. Mara's own face looked blurred around the edges, as if the glass itself refused to know her. She brushed her teeth with the small paper-wrapped brush they'd given her, tasting mint and something chalky. Leah stood beside her but didn't speak again. Her shoulders were tense. She was afraid to say too much. Mara knew the feeling. It had sunk into her bones the moment they crossed the threshold.

After breakfast—which tasted of boiled oats and bitter fruit slices—they were led into a bright room with high windows and a woven rug at the center. The rug was round, embroidered with muted flowers and birds, and every girl took a spot around it as if drawn there by invisible strings. Annora entered through a door that made no sound when it opened. She carried a notebook and a teacup.

"Good morning, my lilies," she said, her voice warm but too rehearsed. "Today, we reflect."

The girls murmured a greeting in unison. "Good morning, Miss Annora."

Mara said nothing.

Annora's gaze slid to her, but didn't linger. She placed the notebook on a side table, then gestured toward a small writing desk by the window.

"You each have your journals. You know what to do."

Mara received hers without ceremony. It had her name embossed in silver script: *Mara Ellison.* Beneath it, in smaller letters: *Grace Through Growth.*

She opened it. The first page was blank. The second bore a typed instruction:

"Today, write about a time you failed to be gentle. How can softness save you next time?"

Mara stared at the words for a long time. Then she picked up the pen, wrote a single sentence, and shut the book.

Sometimes the world deserves the scream.

After journaling, the girls were dismissed with another bell—this one softer, almost soothing, as if the House itself approved of their reflections. Mara held her book tightly, resisting the urge to tear out the page she had written. She could still feel Annora's eyes somewhere behind her.

They returned to the common room, where sunlight pooled too politely across every surface. It was painted in warm neutrals, filled with armchairs and shelves lined with books no one ever seemed to read. A large painting of lilies hung above the fireplace, their white petals splayed open like they were screaming in silence.

A girl with honey-colored braids sat at the piano. She played the same three notes over and over again—soft, hypnotic. The room should've felt peaceful. It didn't.

Mara noticed it then. The bed across from hers, which had been neatly made that morning, was now stripped bare. The trunk at its foot was gone. The photograph clipped to the headboard—a girl with sharp cheekbones and green eyes—had vanished too.

She nudged Leah, who had curled up in a nearby armchair, legs tucked underneath her.

"Hey. Did someone leave?"

Leah didn't respond at first. Her gaze flickered briefly to the empty spot, then back down to her hands.

"You're not supposed to ask," she whispered.

Mara frowned. "Why not?"

"Because she was probably disruptive. And it's better not to dwell on those who didn't want to be helped."

"But—"

Leah leaned closer, her voice lower now. "It's how they test us. You ask too many questions, and they label you unwell. And if you're unwell... you go upstairs."

Mara followed her gaze. A spiral staircase wound upward to a hallway no one ever entered during the day. She hadn't noticed it before.

"What's *upstairs*?" she asked.

Leah didn't answer. She only looked away.

That night, Mara couldn't sleep. The silence was too thick, like it pressed down on the walls and lungs. Across from her, Leah's breathing was steady but shallow. The other beds were still. She didn't know most of their names yet. It felt wrong to ask.

She turned to face the window. Outside, the world was still, but the garden lights were always on, casting long, perfect shadows of rose bushes that never moved in the wind.

Then she heard it.

Not a scream.

A *whimper*. Muffled, rhythmic. From behind the wall.

Mara sat up slowly. The room stayed quiet, but the sound continued. Not loud. Just wrong. A sound that didn't belong in a place that taught girls to speak only in kindness.

She slipped from her bed, feet touching the cold tile, and crept toward the source. The wall by the headboard. She pressed her ear against it.

The sound stopped.

Just as she turned back to her bed, another noise cut through the quiet. A hum.

High-pitched. Mechanical. And then, a second voice—a *girl's voice*—repeating softly:

"I failed to be gentle.
I will be still.
I will be sweet.
I will be still.
I will be sweet."

Over. And over.

Mara's blood ran cold. It wasn't the words.

It was the way the voice *cracked* on the last line. The way it didn't sound like belief.

It sounded like begging.

CHAPTER II

Sometimes the world deserves the scream.
Even if it echoes back as silence.
Even if it's the last sound I ever make.

Mara knew something was wrong the moment the bell rang for breakfast and the doors didn't open.

The girls stood lined up in the hallway like obedient paper dolls, hands clasped in front of them, backs straight, heads tilted slightly down—not too much, just enough to show humility, not fear. That had been a lesson on day one.

But now, the hallway was silent, save for the faint click of Annora's heels.

She appeared at the far end, dressed in dove gray, her expression unreadable—except for her eyes. They were alight with something Mara couldn't name. Not quite anger. Not quite joy. But definitely satisfaction.

"Girls," she began, "before breakfast, we have an opportunity for reflection."

Mara didn't move, but she felt it. The shift. The subtle inhale from Leah beside her. The sudden stillness in Faye.

Annora raised a folded slip of paper in her hand. White. Thin. Torn from a journal.

"In this House, we are taught gratitude. Softness. Growth." She began walking, slow and steady, her voice poised like a thread held over flame. "We prune the parts of ourselves that are unruly. And we do not scream."

She stopped directly in front of Mara.

"This was found during routine journal reviews," she said, her eyes never leaving Mara's face. "A line written without context. But context is not required when the sentiment itself is poison."

Annora unfolded the slip and read aloud, her voice smooth as velvet draped over knives.

"Sometimes the world deserves the scream."

Gasps stirred down the line of girls like a breeze through reeds.

Annora smiled, gently. "Tell me, Miss Ellison... who taught you that the world *deserves* anything but your obedience?"

Mara didn't answer. Her fists tightened at her sides, nails biting into skin. Leah's hand brushed her knuckles—quick, fleeting, a warning or a comfort, she didn't know.

"Well?" Annora prompted.

"It was a feeling," Mara said. "Not a manifesto."

Annora tilted her head. "You misunderstand. Feelings are never *just* feelings, dear girl. They are seeds. And if we let the wrong ones grow..."

She gestured. Two attendants appeared from behind a side door, dressed in white. Expressionless.

"You've been chosen for Reflection Chores," Annora said softly. "Three days. Red Wing."

Mara didn't look at Leah. She didn't look at Faye.

She looked straight ahead and said, "Do I get to scream there?"

Annora's smile didn't falter. "Oh, my dear. No one hears you in the Red Wing."

They took her through the servant's corridor, a back route she hadn't seen before. The walls here were stripped of art. The lights flickered, not because they were broken, but because they were meant to.

Intentional disrepair. A different kind of design.

The Red Wing was colder. That was the first thing Mara noticed. No heating vents, no artificial sunlamps. Just long, bare halls and a door at the end that looked like it had never been opened gently.

The attendant unlocked it with a key that looked too old to belong here. Then they nudged her inside without a word.

The room was vast. Shadowed. There were no windows. Just a faint buzz in the ceiling like something was always watching.

In the corner, a mop and a bucket. On the floor, faint stains—long since scrubbed, but never quite erased.

She heard humming.

Not music. Not from a person.

From the walls.

She stepped forward. Her shoes echoed sharply, like her presence was a violation.

Then—movement.

From a side chamber, a girl appeared. She was small. Pale. Her eyes didn't focus. Her uniform was clean, but wrinkled, like she'd been sleeping on the floor.

Mara opened her mouth, but the girl raised a finger to her lips and whispered,

"They *listen* here."

Mara nodded slowly. "Who are you?"

The girl blinked. "I used to be Faye's partner. Before Faye passed."

Mara's blood turned to frost.

"She's not—"

The girl tilted her head. "She passed. Her Harmony Report. Not the one you're writing. The one she *was*. That's what they say when they reset you."

Mara took a step back.

The girl only smiled. It was too wide.

"They prune the parts that scream."

The door slammed shut behind Mara. A finality that settled into her bones like cold iron.

She turned to the girl again. Pale. Still smiling, still slightly wrong.

"You said Faye passed," Mara said. "But she's not—she was just with me. In the solarium."

The girl's head tilted like a broken marionette. "Yes. That was her post-passing self. A harmony version."

"That doesn't mean anything."

"It means everything."

The girl's eyes darted toward the ceiling, then the corners, then the floor. Like she was scanning for invisible threads, strings that pulled her mouth open or shut.

"You don't understand yet," she whispered, taking slow steps backward. "But you will. You've got three days. That's when the tests begin."

"What tests?"

"You'll see."

Mara took a sharp breath. "Why are you here? Who are you?"

The girl paused in the doorway of a side room—just shadow beyond. "I help. That's my role now. I used to be loud like you. Now I whisper."

And then she was gone. Just like that. No footsteps. No door creaking. Just absence.

Day One in the Red Wing smelled like bleach, old dust, and forgotten stories.

Mara scrubbed floors that didn't look dirty. She wiped walls that already gleamed. Everything was spotless, yet she was told to clean it again.

There was no schedule. No meals unless someone brought them—someone she never saw. Just a tray that appeared when her back was turned.

Time bent weird here.

She thought about that girl. About what she said.

Harmony version.

Post-passing.

A test.

And Faye. A name on a list. A girl with a sharp profile and sharper silence. Yesterday she had glared at Mara like she'd committed a crime just by breathing the same air.

Was she different now?

Or had something been rewritten behind her eyes?

By evening, Mara sat curled under a thin blanket, back pressed against a radiator that didn't hum. Her journal was in her lap. The pages were still there, but one line was missing.

The scream line. Gone. As if it had never been written.

She pressed her pencil to the paper and wrote:

If I vanish, don't believe I went quietly.

Then, new writing—faint and shaky—began to appear beneath hers.

Not her hand.

"Some of us still scream. Just... not out loud."

Mara's blood ran cold.

She slammed the journal shut.

She woke to voices she couldn't place. Echoes behind walls. Whispers that sounded like names.

They gave her a new task: empty the bin in Room B-12.

She wasn't told where that was. Just given a black key and a polite nod.

She wandered until the hallway numbers faded into red paint, then back into blank.

Finally, she found it.

Room B-12.

The key turned.

Inside—rows of beds. Thin sheets. A silence that was *waiting.*

But the bin? Full of shredded paper.

Mara knelt, hands trembling as she sorted through pieces.

Words. Sentences. All cut through like someone had tried to erase memory itself.

She found one jagged scrap with half a line:

...she said the mirror showed her someone else...

And another:

...don't drink the lavender tea...

And then:

Harmony is the lie that eats you from the inside.

Mara sat back hard on the floor.

Her journal burned in her pocket. But she didn't take it out. Not yet.

That night, she found the girl again.

In the washroom, standing in front of the cracked mirror, running her fingers over her face like she wasn't sure it belonged to her.

"You found the paper," the girl said without looking at her.

"What happened to you?" Mara asked, voice soft now. Not defiant. Curious.

"Same thing that happens to all of us. They break you open. Then they sort what's left. Some girls they rebuild. Others—they shelve. I was shelved."

Mara frowned. "But why let you wander? Why tell me things?"

The girl finally looked up, and for a moment, her eyes were lucid. Clear.

"Because you're not afraid yet. And they hate that."

Mara woke up to a new uniform folded at the edge of her bed.

White. Spotless. Crisp.

A note beside it: *Be ready by nine. She is coming.*

She didn't know who *she* was, but her gut curled at the formality.

She dressed.

At 9:00 sharp, the door opened. Not by a guard. Not by the attendants.

By Annora.

She stepped inside like the air bent to make room for her. No heels this time. Barefoot, but still regal. Her presence too large for the space.

"Well," she said, eyeing Mara up and down. "You've learned a few things, haven't you?"

Mara didn't respond.

Annora smiled. "Good. Some questions are meant to be answered in silence. It keeps the mind sharp."

She turned and walked, trusting Mara would follow.

She did.

They reached a chamber Mara hadn't seen before. A room of mirrors. Floor to ceiling. No doors visible. No lights—yet the whole space glowed.

Annora motioned for her to enter.

Mara stepped in.

The mirrors shimmered.

And in each reflection, she saw a different version of herself.

One was weeping. One was laughing. One sat perfectly still, staring back.

But only one—the one in the center—leaned forward, pressed a finger to the glass, and mouthed:

"Run."

The lights snapped off.

CHAPTER III

"If I'm still me... why don't I feel like it?"

Mara woke with a jolt, heart thudding against her ribs like it was trying to flee. The dormitory was still, a pale stream of morning light cutting across the wall beside her bed. Leah stirred in her sleep, murmuring something unintelligible before going quiet again. Mara sat up, every inch of her skin buzzing with the strange discomfort of waking from a dream she couldn't remember—only that it had felt like drowning in silk.

She reached for her journal. Not because she had something to say, but because writing had become the only thing that still made sense. Her thoughts were knots and whispers now, fraying at the edges. The words kept them tethered.

She uncapped her pen and wrote, "Sometimes I wonder if I'm imagining this. Maybe they've already gotten inside me. Maybe I'm starting to believe them." She hesitated, tapping the pen against the paper. Then added, "Is that how it happens? You don't notice the rot until it's underneath your fingernails?"

She stared at the page, her own words breathing back at her in silence. It stayed still. Empty. She flipped to the next page, almost compulsively now, as if her body moved before her brain could stop it. Her breath hitched.

There, in slanted handwriting that was most certainly not hers:

"It's not imagination if we both feel it."

The book snapped shut in her hands with a sound too loud for the quiet morning. She glanced over—Leah was still asleep. Her chest rose and fell steadily. No witnesses. No prank. Just Mara and a page that replied.

She opened the book again slowly, heart a twitching thing in her throat. The ink was still there. Same scrawl, same placement. Not smudged. Not printed. Written. *By what?* Her skin prickled.

She turned the page. Blank. Blank. Blank. Nothing waiting for her. Good. She wrote again. Short this time, just to test it.

"What do you want from me?"

No reply.

She stared at it for five minutes, maybe more. Nothing appeared. She laughed—bitter, a cracked porcelain sound. Tossed the journal into her drawer and slammed it shut. She wouldn't look again. Not today.

11

By breakfast, the ache behind her eyes hadn't gone away. Everything tasted like chalk. Even the fruit—bright and pink and too sweet—was hollow. Around her, the other girls chattered gently about weather and books and gratitude. Gratitude was the word of the day. It always was. Gratitude for the order. Gratitude for the silence. Gratitude for Annora, standing like a statue of benevolence near the entrance, nodding at each girl with a smile that never touched her eyes.

Afterward, they were brought to the music room to rehearse their "Harmony Vows." It was less a song and more a chant, wrapped in the illusion of melody. Mara moved her lips in sync with the others but didn't sing. She watched them. Studied how their smiles were too even, how the glances between them were too short. There was something in the air, like perfume made of secrets.

Later, in the journaling room, she stared at the desk, unsure whether to sit. It felt like choosing to jump into a pit and see how deep it went. But she sat. Her hand trembled only slightly as she pulled the journal from her drawer. It was exactly where she left it. Closed. Unbothered. Harmless.

She opened to a fresh page and pressed her pen down.

"Why do I feel more real when I bleed?"

The question stared back at her, black and sharp.

"Is that what they want? Girls who tear themselves open quietly?"

She waited.

Then came the reply.

"They want you to bleed beautifully."

"Quiet suffering is a virtue here."

"Sing while you hurt, and they will call you healed."

The words unraveled across the page one by one, like someone was writing them just out of sight. Her stomach twisted. She swallowed back the bile crawling up her throat and slammed the book shut.

She stood too quickly, chair scraping against the floor, and left the room. She needed air, needed space, needed to walk until her legs remembered what it felt like to carry a person who still made sense.

In the hall, she passed Mira—the quiet girl who always hummed. She was humming now, slicing invisible lines through the air with her fingers. Her lips curled into a gentle smile. Leah appeared at Mara's side.

"Mira used to scream in her sleep," she whispered. "They gave her time in the White Room."

"What's the White Room?" Mara asked.

But Leah only shook her head. "Don't ask. Just don't."

That night, Mara barely slept. Every sound became a shape. Every creak in the walls a whisper. When she finally slipped into unconsciousness, it was filled with flashes of white fabric and mirrors with no reflection. She awoke with her journal pressed to her chest.

She had left it in the drawer. She was sure of it.

She sat up and hurled it across the room, but it landed softly. No noise. Like it wanted to stay near.

The next morning, she approached it cautiously. Opened it with slow fingers. Blank page.

She didn't even think—just started writing.

"I don't believe you're real.

I don't believe this is happening.

I am sane.

I am sane.

I am sane."

This time, the response was cruel in its calm.

"That's what I told myself too."

"Until I wasn't."

Mara's breath hitched. Her pen shook in her grip.

"Who are you?" she scrawled, the ink messy now. "Why are you in my head?"

A pause.

Then: **"You write like me. I liked that. They didn't."**

She threw the journal across the room again, but it didn't make her feel any better.

Because the truth was beginning to form, unspoken but terrible.

She wasn't just losing her grip.

She was *becoming someone else.*

Or someone else was becoming *her.*

And either way, she didn't know how much longer she could keep pretending nothing was wrong.

The journal stayed where it had landed, pages open like it was waiting for her to come back.

Mara didn't.

Not for hours.

She spent the rest of the day drifting. Her body did the motions—meals, study sessions, posture drills—but her mind felt like it was always a half-step behind. Like reality was being fed to her through a filter, and she couldn't tell if it was *them* or *her*.

During the evening routine, while combing her hair before bed, she stared into the mirror above the sink. Her face looked the same. Same skin, same eyes. But it was like staring at a mask. Nothing behind it. No weight. Just features.

She pinched her arm, hard.

Felt it. Good.

Still here.

Still real.

Right?

"You've been quiet," Leah said from the bed. "Bad day?"

Mara nodded, not trusting herself to speak.

"I get those too," Leah whispered. "Try writing it out. Helps me sometimes."

Mara smiled, even though she didn't mean it. "Yeah," she said, "maybe I'll try that."

Midnight found her kneeling on the floor in front of the journal like it was some cursed relic. She hadn't touched it again since the morning. But now, it felt magnetic. Like if she didn't write, the thoughts would eat her alive.

She opened it carefully, slow like the thing might bite.

The page was blank. Of course it was.

She stared at it for a full minute before writing,

"Do you want something from me?"

Another minute.

Another.

Then:

"Don't we always?"

Her throat tightened. "Who is we?" she scribbled, frantic now. "Who are you?!"

Nothing.

"I'm not scared of you," she lied.

The reply came fast.

"Good."

"Fear clouds the mind."

"And you need clarity if you're going to survive here."

She slammed her palm over the page. *Stop. Stop. Stop.* Her heart was a caged thing now, fluttering fast and senseless.

She was losing it.

Right?

That had to be it. She hadn't slept properly in days. The food here was bland. The routine was strict. The environment—controlled. Maybe her brain was just misfiring. That was all.

She got up, backed away from the journal like it had teeth. Climbed into bed and pulled the blanket up over her head like a child hiding from a monster.

But the worst thing was...

Part of her wanted to write back.

She wanted to ask more. To push. To *know*.

Because if the voice in the pages knew what this place really was... maybe it was the only truth she'd get.

The next day, during the garden walk, she asked Annora a question. Just to see what would happen.

"Do you believe people can change?" she asked, careful to keep her tone soft. Curious. Harmless.

Annora smiled. "We don't believe in change, dear. We believe in *refinement*. You're already who you're meant to be. You've just been covered in noise. We help girls find their signal again."

"But what if I like the noise?"

Annora's smile didn't shift. "Then we'll help you understand why you don't."

She returned to the journal that night like she was returning to a battlefield. She didn't write anything at first. Just flipped through the pages.

Half of them were hers.

The rest? She didn't know anymore. Her handwriting? Maybe. Maybe not.

One line stood out—written faintly in the margin of an earlier entry.

"Don't forget your name."

She blinked at it. That line hadn't been there before. She was sure of it.

She wrote below it: "What do you mean?"

A beat.

"They can't take it from you if you remember."

"Take what?"

"You."

Her pulse surged.

"No one's taking me," she wrote.

"Not yet."

She dropped the pen. Closed the book slowly this time.

And whispered to herself, "I'm still me. I'm still me. I'm still me."

But in the quiet hum of the room, she wasn't sure if she believed it anymore.

CHAPTER IV

It watches when I don't.
It waits when I won't.
And it remembers more than I ever wrote.

Mara woke up with the metallic taste of panic melting on her tongue. Not fear—panic. Sharp. Chemical. Her skin was damp, hair stuck to her forehead, the sheets twisted like she'd been clawing through dreams with both hands. She sat up slowly, heart a fist slamming behind her ribs, eyes dragging toward the far wall.

It was still there.

THE WHITE ROOM REMEMBERS.

The words hadn't faded. Neither had the sense that something was watching.

No—*remembering.*

She hadn't told anyone. Not about the journal answering her. Not about the whispers that coiled behind her thoughts like secondhand smoke.

Not about the wall.

And definitely not about *her.*

The pale girl in the red wing.

Nobody mentioned her. No one else even flinched in that hallway. But Mara saw her. Always. Every time they passed the red wing, she caught a flicker—a flash of bleached skin and hair the color of forgotten things.

The girl didn't just look at her.

She *saw* her.

Eyes wide and glassy. Never blinking. Never looking away.

Like a mirror without mercy.

Breakfast blurred. Leah was laughing with the others, untethered by the rot creeping through Mara's brain. Untouched. None of them had been called to the white room. Not like Faye.

And Faye?

Faye had been edited.

She moved like an afterthought. Smiled in grayscale. Spoke in citations. Like someone had scrubbed her soul until it no longer bled.

Before class, Mara cracked open her journal. Her hands were trembling like they were remembering something her brain hadn't caught up to yet.

"Why only me?" she wrote, pen biting the page.

The answer was waiting, coiled and patient.

"Not only. Just first."

She slammed the journal shut. Her heart kicked like it wanted out. This wasn't madness anymore.

It was a *blueprint.*

The day passed like a dare. Every blank wall buzzed like a held breath. Every shadow stretched wrong. And every time Annora smiled, it was too wide, too white—like her teeth had been polished for performance.

The pale girl appeared again. Closer this time. At the end of the hallway, just beyond the light, in the red wing's reach.

But this time, Mara looked harder.

And froze.

Because the face wasn't blank.

It was *familiar.*

Not exactly hers, but almost. Not a twin.

A version.

A reflection dulled and hollowed. Like a Mara that had surrendered. That had been swallowed.

Stripped of all fight. All fire. All her.

Mara's spine prickled.

Was she a ghost? A clone? A premonition?

The question clung to her skin.

That night, after dinner, Mara pushed her luck. She leaned just a little too close to Annora.

"I guess this place is perfect if you enjoy being watched while you sleep," she said, sweet as arsenic.

Annora's mouth twitched, smile sliding off-balance. "We all have our roles, Mara."

Mara tilted her head. "Yeah. And I'm not playing mine."

The punishment came swift and sterile.

Back to the Red Wing.

But this time, Mara *wanted* it.

She needed to see if the girl was real.

She was.

Closer than ever.

Mara stepped forward, drawn by something beneath her ribs. The girl didn't move, but her mouth... did. No sound. Just the shape of words she wasn't allowed to say.

Then—gone.

A door shut her out. Locked.

B-3.

Inside the Red Wing, the air pressed against her lungs, thick with the weight of unspoken thoughts. The walls didn't just memorize—they *murmured*.

Low. Rhythmic. Like something ancient reciting prayers in reverse.

Mara tried to breathe.

The walls exhaled with her.

Or maybe she exhaled with them.

Either way, something was breathing that shouldn't have been.

Time fractured. She couldn't tell how long she wandered, only that when she stumbled out, her heart was a war drum and her thoughts were unraveling thread. But underneath the fear, something clicked.

Cold. Terrible. True.

She wasn't the only one.

She was one of *many*.

This place wasn't built to break girls.

It was built to *build* something else.

And some of them were... prototypes.

She found Leah in the rec room, curled on the yellow couch like nothing had happened. Same paperback. Same dog-eared page no one ever turned. Everything normal.

But Mara felt like a ghost stepping into her own life.

She sat beside her, bones buzzing. "I need you to believe me," she whispered. "Before I finish."

Leah blinked. "Okay..."

"There's a girl in the Red Wing. Pale. Silent. I saw her again. And she—she looked like me. Like a version of me that stopped fighting. No one else sees her. But she's real. Leah, she's real."

Leah's voice was careful. "You've... seen her before?"

"She doesn't blink. Doesn't breathe. She's like a placeholder. And it's not just her. There are others. I can feel it. This place—it's not just watching. It's choosing. Testing us. And when we fit too neatly..."

Her voice cracked.

"It replaces us."

Leah looked at her like she wanted to believe. But she didn't.

"Mara... maybe you're just not trusting. You've never really let yourself *belong* here. Maybe you're seeing monsters because you don't want to see people. This place—it's not perfect, but it's not evil."

Mara stared at her. "You think this is about me not trying?"

Her voice rose, breathless. "You think I'm just some cliché with a rebel complex? That I can't be 'saved' by your perfect routine?"

Leah flinched. Didn't answer.

Mara stood. "You haven't seen what I've seen. There's something wrong here. And I won't let it take me. Or you."

Leah looked back down at her book.

Her hands were shaking.

That night, Mara didn't touch the journal.

She sat beside the window, knees to chest, watching moonlight stretch silver across the floor like spilled secrets. Behind her, Leah slept. Or pretended to. Neither of them said a word.

The silence was sacred.

Almost safe.

Until it wasn't.

Because when she finally glanced down—

The journal was open.

Not rustled. Not flipped.

Just *open.*

Like it had been waiting.

A corner curled upward, eager.

As if the next page already knew what came next.

And across the open page, written in ink that shimmered like oil and *moved* like a living thing, the letters slid into place. They rippled. Crawled. Bled together, then pulled apart.

Three words.

"B-3 is waiting."

And Mara's soul...

remembered.

CHAPTER V

How can I choose anything if everything's already been chosen for me?
Tonight, I saw the truth. And I think the truth saw me too.

The hallway to B-3 wasn't just long—it was devouring. Narrow walls, low ceiling, the kind of space that didn't echo footsteps but absorbed them. Mara moved like smoke, barefoot and careful, the floor cool under her skin. The House was asleep. Or pretending to be. The girls lay curled beneath white sheets, caught in programmed dreams, and the Matrons had vanished into whatever dark little corners they disappeared to after hours. Even the wind had gone still, like it knew not to make a sound tonight.

The door to B-3 stood slightly open. That thin sliver of darkness sliced through her nerves. A trap? A test? An invitation? She pushed it with just two fingers. It opened too easily. Inside, the air was colder—but not the kind of cold that came from drafts or poor insulation. This was the chill of memory, of spaces that hadn't seen sunlight in years. It was the cold of silence, of grief compacted into walls. Time felt thinner in this room, like it had frayed at the edges. And then Mara saw her. The Pale Girl. Not facing her. Just sitting still in a chair too large for her frame, her back straight, her hands resting in her lap like she was pretending to be older, stronger, someone else. But her presence pulsed with something far more ancient. Mara didn't speak. She couldn't. Her tongue felt stitched to the roof of her mouth.

The Pale Girl spoke instead, her voice soft and off-beat, as if someone had slowed it down and pressed rewind. "You're not supposed to be here yet," she said, without turning. "But you are. And so was I." There was something deeply wrong about her tone—something that felt like a secret not meant to be told. Mara's breath caught. The air felt like it had been filtered through old paper and forgotten letters. The Pale Girl rose with no sound at all and walked toward the wall. Not the door. Not a hallway. Just the wall. Then she stepped through it. No ripple. No shimmer. It simply opened for her like it had been waiting. And Mara followed. She didn't ask herself why. She didn't hesitate. It felt like following a memory she hadn't made yet.

The world changed. Not around her. *Inside* her. The floor beneath her feet remained, but the space had twisted. As though she had stepped behind the curtain of reality and found a backstage she wasn't meant to see.

They weren't in the Red Wing anymore. They weren't even in the House. They were somewhere deeper.

Somewhere that watched.

Somewhere that remembered.

Light swirled like fog. Walls stretched into nothing. Voices whispered without mouths. And on every side of her: stories. Girls. Thousands of them. Moving images flickered on invisible screens. Uniforms. Classrooms. Choreographed movements. Smiles too polished. Tea ceremonies. Graduation rings. Obedience disguised as honor. "The obedient graduate," the Pale Girl whispered, and her voice slid beneath Mara's skin like cold water. "They are released. To marry. To serve. To blend." One face bled into another, indistinguishable. All of them with the same vacant grace, the same desperate perfection. Their eyes said nothing. But Mara could hear it now—the same silence that threaded through her mother's voice every time she said, "I love you. I'm doing this to save you." And suddenly, a new projection started. Mara's stomach dropped. It was her mother. Younger. But unmistakable. Sitting like a doll, answering questions with the exact same cadence as the other girls. The same stiff smile. The same eyes, hollowed out and repainted. A graduation ceremony. A handshake. A veil. And then the screen went dark. Mara's fists clenched, but she didn't feel her fingers.

The Pale Girl didn't explain. She didn't need to. Mara *knew*. Her mother had come from this place. Not metaphorically. Literally. This was the reason she was always half-absent, why she flinched at raised voices and froze at questions. She hadn't been protecting Mara—she had been preserving the cage. "Some are sent back into the world as ghosts," the Pale Girl murmured. "Wrapped in silk. Programmed to forget they were ever alive." And Mara asked, barely able to hear her own voice, "What about the ones who didn't obey?" The lights in the space dimmed. The air thickened. The walls began to shiver. And the images changed.

Photos. Blurred out. Class rosters missing names. Faces scratched from memory. Girls tied to beds. Crying in rooms that looked more like cells. And then gone. Not dead. *Erased*. The Archive began to fracture around the edges, like it was struggling to hold so much silence in place. One screen flickered, stuttered, glitched. It showed the dormitory window of Mara's room. But the girl standing inside wasn't Mara.

It was someone else. Familiar. Gone. "Where did they go?" Mara whispered. "Why did no one come for them?" The Pale Girl didn't answer.

Maybe she couldn't. Or maybe there were no words left for the truth. Just more footage. A family. Sitting at a dinner table. A check being handed over. A polite nod. "They were told not to ask," the Pale Girl said finally. "And they didn't." "They just... let them disappear?" "They were paid to forget." Mara felt her whole-body rebel. Her stomach turned. Her pulse raced. Her bones ached. She had always suspected the world was broken—but she hadn't realized just how carefully it had been designed to be. "They were girls no one wanted back," the Pale Girl whispered. "And they made sure they stayed gone." A name blinked across the wall. Just for a second. *MARA.* Then it vanished, like a deleted file. And just as her breath caught in her throat, the space began to change again.

The final wall opened, and this one *breathed.* Pages fluttered. Lights snapped into focus. And in the center stood Sister Annora—not as Mara knew her now, but younger. Angrier. Wild-eyed and barefoot, screaming into the void. A glitch in the machine. A rebel who hadn't yet lost her fire. The Archive labeled her with brutal efficiency: *Test Subject 003. Recalcitrant. Unreformable. Repeated program failure.* She had fought. She had refused to kneel. She had sparked questions in others. And then... she stopped. Not because she gave in. Because she changed the game. She didn't escape. She integrated. She bent herself into the bones of the House and rewrote the rules from inside. "If I can't free myself," her voice echoed from the projection, "I will mold the next generation into women who don't need to fight. Because no one listens to screaming girls. They listen to silence. To obedience. To survival." She hadn't become a warden. She had become the architect. A ghost who programmed ghosts. A designer of the very system she once hated. And the House still obeyed her.

When Mara returned to her room—if you could even call it that—it didn't feel like hers anymore. The walls looked thinner. The floor creaked more loudly. The shadows clung to her. Her journal sat open on her bed. Waiting. Not where she had left it. The ink shimmered like it had just been written. Like it was still bleeding through the page. The letters curled themselves into words she didn't want to read but couldn't look away from

"There are 14 left.One must break the cycle.

Tag, you're it."

She woke with a gasp that didn't belong to her. Air scraped down her throat like she'd swallowed glass. She sat up so fast the world tilted—if it could even be called a world. There were mirrors everywhere. No ceiling. No floor. Just a chair in the middle of a space that wasn't a room but a reflection of one. Every angle of her face caught and twisted and repeated back at her like a thousand versions of herself she didn't recognize. The lighting was sterile, soft and sour, like a dream made of hospital corridors and forgotten intentions. She was alone. For now. And she didn't know who brought her here or why. But something in her gut whispered: *You're not supposed to leave. Not as you came in.*

Her eyes landed on the chair. Wooden. Sharp-cornered. Handmade, maybe even hastily, and with it, a gift: weakness. She bent to the leg, snapped a piece off. It splintered with a scream. And then she turned the jagged end toward her skin. She didn't hesitate. She didn't flinch. Pain was familiar. Pain was hers. They could strip her uniform. Her name tag. Her voice. Her hair. But they wouldn't take *this*. Not again. Not ever. She carved **MARA** into the soft skin of her inner thigh—deep enough to sting, shallow enough not to bleed out, but raw and real. It burned like truth. It throbbed like memory. She hissed between her teeth, grit her jaw, and whispered, "You can forget me. But I won't."

The mirrors stared back. Silent. Shimmering. Judging. And then one moved. No, *opened.* A slit of light. A breath of something colder. And from the reflection stepped Sister Annora like the ghost of every unlearned lesson, spine straight and eyes hard as porcelain. No empathy. No performance. Just clinical disappointment served cold. "I should've taken you more seriously," she said, tone brittle and bored. "But you never struck me as the dangerous kind. A quiet file. Clean scores. Polite defiance. I thought you'd fold like the others." Her boots clicked softly against the mirrored floor. Mara's hands clenched around the wooden shard like a prayer.

"But after all these years," Annora continued, circling, "*you're* the one who defied me. You went behind my back. You saw what you weren't supposed to see. Did you think I wouldn't know? I have eyes in every corner of this House. I hear everything." She stopped behind Mara. "And now... so will you." Without warning, she yanked Mara's arms behind her. The wooden shard was ripped from her hand. The pain barely registered. Annora moved with the precision of someone who had done this before. Rope slithered around Mara's wrists, binding her to the very chair she had drawn power from. Ironic. Or poetic. Or both. Mara fought, not to get free—she knew better than to waste strength—but to keep the flame inside her from flickering out.

"You'll sit here," Annora whispered, her voice suddenly intimate, cruel in its calmness, "and you'll reflect on everything you've done to not deserve this kind world." She produced a pair of shears from beneath her robe. Cold steel caught the mirrored light. Mara didn't have time to brace herself. With a brutal swipe, Annora dragged the blades through her hair. Again. Again. Until it fell in clumps, scattering around her feet like dead things. Like everything soft they wanted gone. "We strip away the parts that misbehave," Annora murmured, almost to herself. "And then we offer them back, cleansed." She stepped away. Mara sat, bound, bleeding, bare.

Then came the ice. A block, solid and cruel, slid beneath her feet. It crackled against her skin like judgment. "You will stay here," Annora said, adjusting the ropes so Mara's ankles dug into the ice, "until this melts. Until *you* melt. Until you find the warmth in you and give it to the world. Only then will you leave. And if not... well. Some girls never do." She paused at the door. "We will see who you are when no one's looking."

And then she was gone. The mirror door shut with a hiss. No lock clicked. Because it didn't need to. No one escapes a prison made of themselves. Mara sat alone. Her breath visible in the cold. Her name stinging in her skin. Her scalp bare. Her feet burning. Surrounded by her own reflection.

And not one of them looked away.

CHAPTER VI

There was no sleep, only the slow unraveling of time. The ice beneath Mara's feet had long since melted, leaving behind a puddle that seeped into her skin like shame. The chill had sunk into her bones, taken root in her teeth, in her lungs. Every breath tasted like frost and failure.

The mirrors didn't just reflect anymore.

They whispered.

At first, it was just her name. Mara. Mara. Soft as breath, sharp as teeth. Then came the others. Faces. Shifting, mutating, flickering in the reflections like moths caught in amber. Girls she didn't know. Girls she almost remembered. Girls with her eyes, her mouth, her mother's smile.

"Why didn't you run faster?"

"You always thought you were different."

"She warned you."

"You should've shut up."

"You're not brave. Just loud."

She tried to shut them out, but the voices didn't stop. They overlapped, tangled, grew louder until they were inside her skin. And then her own voice joined them—fractured, frightened, begging.

Let me go. I'll be good. I'll be better. I'll disappear.

One mirror split like a wound.

And from it, the Pale Girl stepped.

Her feet didn't touch the ground. Her eyes didn't blink. Her presence made Mara's breath hitch and catch like a cough that never finished.

"You still have a way out," the Pale Girl whispered. "If you dare."

But Mara couldn't dare. She couldn't think. She couldn't feel her hands. Her head pounded with voices that weren't hers, that might've always been hers. She was freezing. She was burning. She was unraveling like thread cut too short.

"There is no door," Mara whispered back. "There's just this."

And then she gave up.

She slumped into the chair like a marionette with its strings sliced through. Her scalp burned. Her thighs ached where her name pulsed red and raw. The chair held her like it knew her, like it was meant for her.

Darkness arrived without warning, without comfort.

She collapsed.

And woke.

In her room.

Warm.

Dry.

Safe.

Safe?

The mirrors were gone. The rope burns had faded. Her hair was gone, still—just fuzz now. But the pain was... distant. Like it had happened to someone else. Like maybe she'd dreamed it.

The journal lay open on her desk.

Empty.

Except for one line.

"Good girls survive."

Mara stared at the words until they blurred. And then she smiled.

Not because she believed it.

But because she knew now what they needed to see.

She stood, slow and deliberate. Smoothed her uniform. Lowered her gaze in the mirror above the desk.

When breakfast was called, she stepped out of the room with perfect posture.

She curtsied when spoken to.

She thanked the Matron for her kindness.

She joined in reciting the morning vows with just the right inflection.

And when they smiled at her?

She smiled back.

Because she'd finally learned the most important lesson the House could teach.

To take back control... you must let them think they have it.

CHAPTER VII

They say the best girls are the ones who listen. But listening doesn't mean believing.

She smiled more now. Not too wide. Not too eager. Just enough to look like she'd been... changed. Softened. Broken in the "right" places and then glued back together with their glue. Like something inside her had snapped clean and now she was finally in tune with the melody the House hummed. A melody made of submission and silence and the sweet, dulled sighs of girls who no longer fought.

Mara sat straighter in her lessons, hands folded just right, chin tilted at the angle that said: I understand now. She answered when spoken to. She laughed gently when the Matrons made their strange brittle jokes. She thanked them for the bland food, complimented their tea like it wasn't steeped in obedience. She bowed her head when Annora passed in the hall, and when the Warden offered her that faint, assessing smile, Mara returned it with one of her own—a careful, mirror-perfect mimicry of the ones she'd seen carved onto the graduates' faces.

She fetched tea without being told. Polished silver until it gleamed. Memorized the names of the Matrons and recited them with reverence. When Annora needed someone to deliver the daily scrolls or collect the unsmiling mail from the East Wing, it was Mara who was called. Soon she was permitted into the Matron's quarters, a rare privilege whispered about in the dormitories like a myth. There, she swept floors, arranged flowers, folded robes. She saw corners of the House most girls weren't allowed to see. The desk drawers. The locked cabinets. The list—long and yellowing—of which girls would soon graduate, and which would not.

She never lingered. Never touched. Just observed. Every errand became a reconnaissance mission. Every kind word she spoke was a tool. And the more she smiled, the more invisible she became. No one suspects the one who obeys.

Days passed like water. Smooth, silent, never still. And Mara played the part so well that sometimes, in the dark of early morning, she'd lie in her cot and feel herself dissolving. Becoming the thing they wanted. Becoming a perfect echo. And then she'd shift just slightly, her leg brushing against the faint scar on her inner thigh. Her name. Still there. Scraped into her skin by her own hand. Proof she had not been erased. The pain of it had faded now, dulled into a quiet throb that pulsed when the air was cold. But the mark remained. Her private brand. A heartbeat she'd given herself.

Then came the announcement. The bell. The footsteps.

Faye was to graduate.

It was during supper. Everyone froze for a moment, spoons held mid-air, eyes wide. And then the room moved again, as if the moment had never happened. Except it had. Faye was still, blinking slowly like the news hadn't reached her ears yet, even as the other girls reached over to squeeze her hand or offer stiff congratulations.

Mara didn't flinch. She didn't speak right away. She simply reached out and took Faye's hand, gave it a gentle squeeze. Then she smiled. She hugged her. Told her how proud she was. How beautiful she would look in the white graduation dress. Faye's lips trembled slightly, as though she wanted to say something. But then she smiled too.

That night, Mara helped her fold her clothes. They whispered like normal girls. About ribbons and shoes. About how nice it would be to have warm sheets and a real window. Faye never asked Mara what she thought of it all. Perhaps she knew. Perhaps she didn't want to.

When morning came, Mara watched her walk down the long white hallway. Faye wore the dress like a wedding gown, bouquet in hand, shoes too tight. Her hair had been brushed until it shone. She didn't look back.

None of them ever did.

Mara didn't cry. She didn't even sigh. But something inside her sank lower, like a weight had been tied to her ribs. Faye was a painting being moved to another museum. Framed and frozen and never meant to speak again.

She had played the game. Perfectly. And the reward was vanishing.

Later that day, Annora passed Mara in the corridor, touched her shoulder lightly and said, "You are one of my brightest." Her voice was warm. Almost motherly.

Mara smiled.

And behind her eyes, the fire kept burning.

That night, the door creaked open with a hush like a held breath. Mara turned just as Leah stumbled in—barefoot, shaking, her hands fisting the hem of her nightgown like it was the only thing anchoring her to earth.

"They're getting me," Leah gasped.

Mara crossed the room in seconds. "What?"

"They're *in* my room—I—" Her voice cracked. "I can hear them. The whispers. The voices in the walls. I see them in the mirrors. They're watching me, Mara. Watching and *waiting*. And I'm not—I'm not the same. I'm not the girl who walked through those gates. I don't think I'll make it out."

Mara's hands found hers. Cold. Bone-tight. "Hey. Leah. Look at me."

Leah's eyes were wide with something far too old for seventeen. "You were right," she whispered, voice trembling like a spider's thread in a storm. "Back then... when I thought you were slipping. I thought you were mad. But now—I know. I *know*. I believe you. And I need you to save me."

That word. **Save.** It hit Mara like a match struck in a dark place.

"I will," she said. "But we need to be smart. We have one chance to end this. One chance to break the cycle."

Leah nodded through her fear. "Tell me what to do."

Mara leaned in, voice barely air. "You need to misbehave. Make a scene. Not too loud, not too quiet. Just enough to make them lock you in Red Wing."

Leah's eyes widened. "That's where—"

"Where the files are. Where the truth lives." Mara gripped her hand tighter. "They trust me. I'll get us in. And out."

The next day, Leah threw her tray during supper. Not violently. Just enough for the clang to draw sharp glances and Annora's pinched, frostbitten frown. Enough to be labeled *emotionally unbalanced*. Enough to be removed. That night, she was sent to Red Wing under the veil of "reflective rest."

And Mara?

Mara requested to deliver her nightly tea.

That night, Mara walked the corridor with the tray in her hands, steady as ever—calm on the outside, hurricane on the inside. Her steps echoed against the sterile tile, as the aroma of lavender and chamomile rose from the porcelain teacup like a trap wrapped in a lullaby.

The *tea*.

No one ever questioned the tea.

It was tradition. Routine. Sacred, almost. Brewed daily in the East Wing and served every evening to every girl—always with a smile, always with a word of comfort. *It helps you rest. It helps you reflect. It helps you heal.*

No one told them it also helped you **forget.**

Mara hadn't known at first. No one ever did. But weeks of shadowing Annora had opened doors not just to locked rooms—but to locked truths. Annora had called it the *Elixir of Serenity*. A delicate blend of herbs... and something else. Something you didn't taste but always felt: the slipping of thoughts, the fuzzing of focus, the gentle tilt of reality.

A psychoactive compound. Low dose. Just enough to dull the fight.

To keep them docile.

Suggestible.

Obedient.

Leah had once described her evenings after tea as *like trying to dream with your eyes open*. And Mara knew now—she hadn't been poetic. She'd been under the spell.

Annora had explained it once, almost proudly. "Some girls," she said while carefully measuring the powder, "are too tightly wound. They cling to trauma like armor. This helps peel it back. Makes them easier to... guide."

Guide. What a word.

What a lie.

And now, Mara carried that same tainted tea to Leah.

Except tonight, it was different.

Mara had spent the week learning the process. Watched how the compound was stored in a tiny brown vial. Watched how the Matron diluted just enough of it into the steeping water. How too much would make them blackout, too little and they might notice the absence.

Mara had perfected the measure. But tonight, she brewed Leah's cup *without it*.

No powder. No fog. No leash.

Just lavender and a whisper of hope.

When she reached the Red Wing, the security guard didn't blink. Just unhooked the keys from his belt and nodded. "Of course," he said. "She trusts you most."

The lock clicked open.

Inside, Leah sat on the edge of the cot, her knees drawn up, eyes alert. Not cloudy. Not slowed.

Mara set the tray down and passed the cup to her.

Leah exhaled like she hadn't in days. "Thank you."

They wasted no time. As Leah drank, Mara moved to the far wall, where a loose panel hid the secondary keys. She'd seen Annora use it once during a sudden inspection. It was how the Matrons accessed the archive room without alerting security.

That part of the story you know.

They found the *Deceased* drawer.

They found the lies—the ones printed neatly in black ink, filed alphabetically by first name.

They found the hush money agreements, signed with trembling hands by parents who never got to bury their children properly.

They found the silence, thick and archived, sold at a high price in the name of "protection."

And then, they found *her*.

Lana.

She was in the file labeled simply *L – 0031*.

Twelve years old. Pale skin. Faint freckles. A photo clipped to the top right corner—black-and-white, taken just weeks before her file was sealed.

Date of birth.

Date of death.

Cause: *Undisclosed psychological collapse.*

Treatment status: *Terminated.*

But there was a note in Annora's handwriting, more intimate than the others:

"Lana was delicate. But she needed to understand that discipline is love."

Mara felt the blood drain from her face.

She reread it. Once. Twice.

"Is this...?" Leah's voice was a whisper that trembled like glass about to shatter.

Mara nodded slowly. "Her daughter."

Leah reeled back. "She—killed her own daughter?"

"No," Mara said quietly, voice brittle. "She tried to *fix* her. And when that didn't work... she erased her."

They didn't speak again. They didn't need to.

They just moved.

They stuffed every file they could into the false-bottom compartment of Mara's bag. Leah slipped a few into the lining of her jacket, taping them against her skin with trembling fingers. Girls who had vanished. Girls who had died. Girls whose parents were paid to keep their grief quiet. Every secret had a paper trail—and they were going to carry it out on their backs like stolen ghosts.

They made it back to Red Wing just before the patrol shift change. Mara returned the key. Leah slipped back into her cot.

The guard locked the door behind her with a casual grunt.

To everyone else, nothing had happened.

To them, *everything* had.

But nothing at Briarhall stayed quiet for long.

By morning, the air had changed. Not visibly. Not obviously. But Mara *felt* it. Like a static charge in the bones. A wrongness. A weight.

Annora was smiling more than usual. Her praise, sweeter. Her gaze, heavier.

And then it came.

After breakfast, Leah was summoned. No reason given. Just a note in Annora's cursive:

"White Room. She's ready."

Mara's breath caught behind her ribs.

No.

Not yet.

They weren't ready.

Leah hadn't seen the exit maps. They hadn't figured out the camera rotations. They hadn't even made backup copies of the files yet.

She watched as two Matrons flanked Leah like wolves in pressed uniforms, gently urging her away from the dining hall. Leah didn't fight. She didn't cry. She just turned her head slightly—and for a second, her eyes locked with Mara's.

They didn't say anything. Couldn't.

But Leah's eyes said enough: *Trust you. Believe you. Please.*

Mara wanted to scream. Wanted to tear the walls down.

But she didn't.

Because Annora was watching.

Because she had to stay perfect.

Because the moment Mara slipped, it would all fall apart.

So she smiled. Just like they'd trained her.

She poured the tea. Just like always.

She offered her arm to Annora, and walked with her through the garden, discussing the spring bloom schedule.

But inside?

Inside, Mara was unraveling.

Her every breath was a war cry muted by lips trained to smile. Her every step toward Annora was a step closer to fire. Her every heartbeat screamed Leah's name.

Because trust wasn't just weaponized anymore.

It was a countdown.

And they were running out of time.

CHAPTER VIII

This room doesn't build anything. It buries.
And today... I'm supposed to help dig.

They gave her the assignment like it was a gift. A privilege. An honor.
"Go accompany Leah for her final transition," Annora said, her voice like a melody wrapped in poison. "She's always responded best to you. It would be... symbolic."

Mara kept her face smooth. Grateful.

Inside, something in her cracked and curled into itself.

She knew what "final transition" meant.

First, the lavender tea—dosed enough to blur the edges of the world.

Then, the stripping. The cleansing.

And then, the ritual.

Hair shaved clean. Bare feet placed on the ice block, to "remind the body of its fragility and its strength."

All under the silver eye of the surveillance camera.

All under Annora's gaze.

Mara walked the long hallway to the White Room with her hands folded, her steps even.

But her soul?

Her soul was screaming.

When the heavy door opened, the room bloomed into clinical light—too white, too bright, too sterile to hold any form of mercy.

And in the center of it—on a stool too small for comfort—was Leah.

Her hands were in her lap. Her shoulders hunched.

And her face...

Tears streaked her cheeks like ink bleeding across paper. Her lips were trembling. Her hair, still long, was damp at the ends.

Mara stepped in and closed the door behind her.

"Leah," she breathed.

Leah looked up slowly. Her eyes were red, swollen, raw.

"I don't want to do this anymore." Her voice was hollow. "I can't. I'm not like you, Mara. I'm not strong."

"You *are*," Mara said instantly, crossing the room to kneel before her. "You're the strongest person I know."

Leah shook her head violently. "No. No, I'm not. I'd rather die than let them change me. I'd rather throw myself through that window than come out of here empty, clean, erased. I *feel* myself slipping already. I saw a girl in the mirror this morning and she didn't look like me. She didn't even flinch. Mara, I don't want to be *that*."

Mara grabbed her hands. Held them like lifelines. "Listen to me. Listen." She forced Leah to meet her eyes. "You won't be that. You won't. Because I'm going to get you out of here. I *swear it.*

You just have to hold on a little longer. Please. Don't do anything reckless. Not now. Not when we're so close."

"But it hurts," Leah whispered. "All the time. Inside. My memories... they don't feel like mine anymore. I can't even hear my own thoughts without doubting if they're real or if someone planted them there. I feel like I'm vanishing."

Mara pulled her into a hug so tight, it felt like an anchor.
"I won't let you disappear," she murmured into her hair. "You're all I have left. We were just kids, remember? Playing in the storm drains behind my house, trying to catch frogs and making those stupid flower crowns."

"You always made me wear yours," Leah sniffled.

"Because they were ugly and I needed someone brave enough to rock them," Mara laughed softly. Then quieter, with more ache: "We weren't supposed to end up here. But we found each other again. That has to mean something. I would always choose you, Leah. Over and over. Even if the whole world turned to fire—I'd walk through it for you."

Leah sobbed into her shoulder.

"You're my family," Mara whispered. "Maybe not by blood. But in every way that counts."

And then, because the camera was watching, she stood.
Tears blinked away. Composure forced back into place.

She placed the silver ice block on the white tile.
The chill bit through her gloves.

"Ready?" she asked gently.

Leah nodded, silent.

She stepped onto the block barefoot.
And as the cold seeped into her bones, Mara leaned in and whispered:

"Golden hour. Field of flowers. You'll make me a crown, and we'll read *Jane Eyre.* Just hold on, okay? Trust me. We'll be okay."

And then she walked out of the White Room.

She left her heart behind.

That night, the halls were drenched in their usual hush. The Matrons had retired. The girls were medicated and dreaming strange, foggy dreams.

Mara's breath was steady as she crept through the east wing.

She picked the lock to Annora's office with shaking hands. The click was a thunderclap in the silence.

Inside, papers rustled like they knew they weren't supposed to be touched.

She found it.

The map.

Taped beneath Annora's desk.

A hidden emergency route. An escape.

We're going to make it, she thought, gripping it like salvation.

She stepped out into the hallway.

And that's when it started.

The alarm.

Not just a light.

Not just a bell.

But a *siren.*

From the White Room.

Mara froze.

No.

No alarms ever rang from the White Room.

Girls went in. Girls came back. But it was always... silent.

She ran.

Instinct moved her faster than breath.

Her legs burned. Her lungs begged.

Other doors opened. Matrons spilled into the hall.

And then Mara saw her.

Annora.

Walking toward the same direction.

But her face...

That smile.

That strange, flickering thing that didn't belong to any emotion Mara had ever learned to name.

Even *Annora looked scared.*

They entered the White Room together.

And there—

There she was.

Leah.

Her body, still.

So pale.

So heartbreakingly still.

Her limbs curled delicately, like a doll set down mid-play and forgotten.

Her eyes—closed.

Her lashes resting on cheeks that no longer held warmth.

No breath.

No flicker of life beneath the thin skin of her throat.

No sound.

Just... the silence.

That horrible, dense, suffocating silence.

Something shattered inside Mara—something ancient and sacred and already cracked from years of pretending she was fine.

Her legs buckled before she realized they'd moved. She collapsed to the tile with a dull, echoing thud, the cold biting her knees.

Her heart was screaming, but her mouth couldn't keep up. Her lips moved, but no sound came out.

She reached for Leah's hand with trembling fingers.

And oh God—

It was cold.

Not the kind of cold that passes.

The kind of cold that stays.

The kind of cold that means it's *too late*.

"No. No. No—" she whispered, her voice breaking on each syllable. "We were going to leave. You promised me. You *promised*. We had a plan. We—we had everything..."

The tears came hard and fast, slipping down her cheeks like rain on stone, like grief carving its name into her skin.

"I told you to wait for me," she choked out. "I *told* you I'd save you. I said we'd make it out of here. I swore it. I meant every word."

She cradled Leah's lifeless hand between her own, trying to rub warmth into it, as if she could undo it all, as if she could turn back time with touch alone.

She leaned forward until her forehead pressed against Leah's.

And her whole body—every breath, every heartbeat, every cell—ached.

"I need you," she whispered into that too-quiet room. "You were the only reason I could breathe in this place.

You were the only part of this hell that ever felt like home. You—"
Her voice broke completely.
"I can't do this without you. I *can't*."
And still, Leah didn't move.
Didn't blink.
Didn't breathe.

She was gone.

But the room didn't feel empty.
No.
It felt full.
With grief. With rage. With the ghost of all the things they never got to say.
The flower crown she'd never get to braid.
The field they'd never lie in, bathed in golden hour light.
The pages of *Jane Eyre* they'd never read aloud.

Gone.

And Mara—
She didn't scream.
She didn't lash out.
She didn't punch walls or flip over chairs.

She broke quietly.
Like a vase sliding off a high shelf, shattering in slow motion.
A collapse you don't even hear until your chest is already aching.

She wept into Leah's neck, her body shaking like something untethered from gravity.
"I'm so sorry," she whispered again and again. "I should've been faster. I should've known. I should've stayed."

She didn't care who was watching.
Didn't care that the Matrons stood frozen behind her.
Didn't care that Annora hadn't spoken a word, only stood there with that tight, unnatural smile fading into something uglier.

Because this was *it*.
This was the worst thing Mara Ellison had ever felt.

And she knew—without a doubt—she would never, ever be the same again.

CHAPTER IX

Something inside me is gone. And what's left behind... doesn't weep anymore. It waits.

The dormitory was too quiet.

Grief doesn't sound like wailing. Not always. Sometimes, it sounds like absence. Like breath held too long. Like a heartbeat that forgets what to do next.

Mara sat on her bunk, Leah's bunk now stripped bare across from hers—mattress empty, sheets gone, pillow missing. They had erased her like a name from the registry. But not from Mara. Never from Mara.

Her hands trembled in her lap. She hadn't spoken since the night the alarm rang from the White Room. Since she saw Leah's lifeless body, pale and small, like she had been carved from cold porcelain. Since she pressed her forehead to hers and whispered broken promises into her cooling skin.

She hadn't cried after that—not in front of them. Not where they could see. She couldn't. Annora watched her like a hawk circling something almost dead. As if she knew grief was dangerous. As if Mara might weaponize it.

And maybe she would.

Because inside Mara now was nothing but shards.

And somewhere among them, something was sharpening.

The next morning, the dormitory door groaned open like it was in pain.

A shadow cut through the hallway light, trailing behind it the sickly perfume of wilted lilies and falseness. Girls paused, heads turning—half from curiosity, half from instinct. Someone important. But the moment Mara lifted her head and saw the silhouette, her stomach twisted into a cold, iron knot.

It wasn't Annora.

It was Leah's mother.

And she looked nothing like grief.

Her heels clicked against the tile like the ticking of a countdown. Her black dress was too polished, her gloves too smooth, her veil too sheer to hide the sharpness in her eyes. She wore sorrow the way some wore perfume—sprayed on just enough to pass, but never strong enough to convince.

Mara's breath stilled in her throat.

She had seen monsters before. But there was something uniquely horrifying about the ones that called themselves family.

The woman didn't hesitate. "I need to speak with Mara," she said, her voice slicing through the silence like a scalpel. Cold. Controlled.

The matron hesitated. Just a breath. Then nodded.

Mara stood because she was called—not because she wanted to. Her feet felt heavy. Her bones, hollow.

Leah's mother turned to her like she was assessing a stain on her coat. "You're the one who brought her here."

It wasn't a question.

Mara's spine straightened, instinct sharpening her voice. "She asked me to."

"She was a child."

"She didn't know what she wanted."

"She knew exactly what she didn't want," Mara said, a spark flickering in her chest. "You."

The woman's nostrils flared, but her voice didn't rise. It dropped lower, quieter. "Then I hope you're happy."

Mara stared, her mouth tightening. "Excuse me?"

"I hope you're satisfied," she said, stepping closer, the perfume of wealth and rot curling in her wake. "You handed her over to this place, and now she's—" Her voice hitched. Just for a second. Not real emotion. A practiced stumble, well-placed. She continued, smoother. "Now she's gone."

Mara's fists clenched at her sides. "You gave her up a long time ago," she said. "All I did was walk her through the doors."

"You think you're so righteous." A cruel smile crept onto her lips. "But tell me, little girl. Do you know what grief looks like?"

Mara's voice came out like frost. "It doesn't look like you."

That struck. For a heartbeat, the woman's expression faltered—before snapping back into place.

"I'll be speaking with the board," she said. "There will be... compensation. They'll understand how deep my pain runs."

Mara blinked, slow. Her voice was steady. Too steady. "You mean hush money."

Leah's mother smiled.

Not the kind of smile you give when someone tells you good news.

The kind of smile you give when you think you've won.

"Sweet girl," she said, brushing a speck of dust from her sleeve like it personally offended her. "You're smarter than you look."

Mara stared at her. Really looked at her.

And suddenly, it all clicked.

This woman hadn't come for closure. She hadn't come for answers. She hadn't even come to pretend she cared.

She came to cash in.

To turn her daughter's death into a dollar sign.

To sell grief the same way this place sold silence.

And just like that, the ache in Mara's chest burned into fury. Quiet, simmering, deadly.

Because Leah never had a mother.

She had a woman who wore the title like a badge but never the weight. A woman who cared more about money than lullabies. Who wouldn't know Leah's favorite book or the way she chewed her thumb nail when she was scared or how she always braided Mara's hair when she couldn't sleep.

"You never deserved her," Mara said, voice low, trembling with truth. "She was brave. She was kind. She made this place bearable. And you never even knew who she was."

Leah's mother rolled her eyes. "Spare me the sentiment. She's gone. That's the only part that matters."

Mara took a step forward, eyes glinting. "She mattered. Every single breath she took mattered. And if you think you're going to walk away from this with your pockets full and your conscience clean—"

"I don't have a conscience," the woman interrupted smoothly.

And that, somehow, was the most honest thing she'd said all morning.

Mara didn't respond. She didn't need to. Because something had shifted. She had seen Leah's mother now. Fully. And she would never forget.

When the woman finally turned and left, her heels echoing like funeral bells, Mara didn't look away.

She watched her until the dormitory doors closed again.

And then she sat back down on her bunk.

And she whispered, to no one, to the girl who wasn't there—

"I'll make sure she never forgets your name."

CHAPTER X

They buried her body. I'll bury their lies.

The day of the funeral arrived dressed in sorrow. The sky itself had dimmed. Clouds draped over the heavens like a mourning shroud, low and unmoving, casting the world in a dull shade of ash. Even the wind seemed unwilling to speak. It simply existed—like Mara.

She stood alone in the hallway of the East Wing, already cloaked in black.

Her dress was long, modest, formal—the kind of thing Leah would have mocked for being too prim, too structured. But it served its purpose. Because stitched into the lining, like veins beneath skin, were stolen secrets. The files. Every single one she and Leah had collected—photocopied, cross-referenced, labeled in red pen. And Lana's folder, the most damning of all. No one knew Mara had sewn a hidden compartment into the dress's folds. No one had suspected her silence might be sharper than their discipline.

She walked past the other girls, who peeked through half-open doors. Their eyes followed her, wide and uncertain. No one was allowed out during a funeral. Not unless the board deemed it appropriate. Which meant not unless you were useful.

Mara was useful now. The sacrificial shadow of the school, paraded out to prove they cared.

She didn't speak to the others. She didn't wave goodbye. She knew better than to give them false hope. Grief in this place was not communal—it was packaged, rationed, hidden behind layers of protocol and prayers.

Even death had a dress code.

The funeral was held on the institution's old grounds, where the trees were sickly and tired. The headstones were all the same size, the same shape, spaced perfectly as if their residents had been arranged like items in a filing cabinet. Leah was given one of the newer plots.

Her headstone was too clean, her name etched in soulless serif font:

Leah Jane R.

2000 – 2017

A Light Lost Too Soon.

Mara wanted to scream at it.

She wasn't just a *light*, she was *a storm*. A riot of color in a monochrome world. A girl with calloused fingers and a laugh that cracked ceilings. Leah had fought for truth like it was oxygen. And now they'd reduced her to a euphemism and an expiration date.

They buried her under a tree that no longer bloomed.

Fitting.

A place that once promised life and now gave only shadow.

Annora stood off to the side, a small distance away. She wasn't watching Leah's grave.

She was standing in front of another.

A smaller one.

Lana's.

Her daughter.

She didn't cry. Of course she didn't. Grief had been bred out of her long ago. But Mara noticed the way her hands lingered against the edges of the grave's stone. The way her thumb brushed over a carved date. The year Lana died: 1992

Mara didn't have to ask why she was there.
She already knew.

Because now she had the proof.

Lana's file—the one marked with the same red stamp as Leah's—sat folded and hidden against Mara's ribs. There were falsified medical records inside. A signed document declaring "complications" as the cause of death. But there was no mention of the drug trial Annora had enrolled her in. No trace of the testing that had accelerated her condition, or the hush money paid afterward to clean the slate.

They all thought the past was buried.

But Mara had learned something in her short, painful time here.

The past doesn't stay buried. Not if you dig hard enough.

The service was quick, sanitized.

A blessing was said by a woman from the board who had never spoken to Leah once.
She mispronounced her middle name.

Mara's eyes didn't leave the ground.

Not until the final *Amen* faded into the overcast sky.

That's when she moved.

Quietly, like a memory leaving the room. She didn't run—running would get her noticed. She simply walked, hands folded, face blank. The files burned against her skin with every step, but she didn't waver.

No one stopped her at the gate.

The guards had been briefed to expect Mara to attend. Her name was on the list. She was *allowed*. And no one in power ever bothered to ask *what else* someone might be doing when they're supposed to be grieving.

The town sat like a forgotten relic just outside the institution's reach. It was small, half-sleeping, dotted with rusted signs and old churches. But Mara didn't go to a sanctuary.

She went to a corner café with fading green awnings.

The journalist was already waiting.

He was older than she expected. Mid-thirties, maybe. Dressed plain. Wary eyes. He stood when she entered and didn't speak at first. He just looked at her—really looked—like he was trying to make sure she was real.

Mara sat and slid the envelope across the table.

Thick.

Heavy with truth.

"I made copies," she said, voice flat.

He nodded. Opened the envelope.

His face changed as he flipped through the pages. Eyes narrowing, then widening. Jaw clenching. His fingers trembled when he saw Lana's file.

"This can't be real," he muttered.

"It is."

"They'll try to shut this down—"

"They've done it before," Mara said. "But this time, it's not just a rumor. There are names. Dates. Signatures. Deaths."

He looked up. "Are you safe?"

"No." A pause. "But I'm done being quiet."

He exhaled like someone who hadn't realized they were holding their breath.

"I'll run it. I'll spread it. I have contacts—forums, independent sources, a legal team. We'll release it in pieces so they can't scrub it all at once. But I need time."

Mara nodded. "Take it. Just make sure it's loud."

He slipped the files into a bag. "It will be. They won't be able to bury this."

Mara stood.

Turned to go.

But then she paused, one hand on the café door. Her voice came soft. Hollow.

"She was my friend."

The journalist looked up again.

"She mattered," Mara whispered. "They'll all try to forget her. Please don't let them."

He didn't smile.

But he did nod.

Like a promise.

By the time the last clump of dirt hit Leah's coffin, Mara was already on her way back to the dormitory.

Back to her cage.

But not as the same girl.

She had walked out quiet.

She returned burning.

The matron barely looked at her when she entered, more concerned with dinner rotations and headcounts. The girls peeked out again. Some asked what the outside looked like. Mara only said it was cloudy.

That night, she sat in her bunk and stared at the ceiling.

She didn't cry.

She didn't speak.

But she smiled, just a little.

Because somewhere, out in the world, Leah's name was being typed.

Her story was being read.

And soon—

Soon the world would finally hear them scream.

Epiligoue

It was spring again.

Not the kind of spring that happened just because a calendar said so, but the real kind. The kind where everything breathes again. Where even things that were broken find a way to bloom.

The girls were safe now.

Every one of them.

They had been sent to shelters, real ones, not cages dressed up as care. Places with warm beds, soft voices, and people who looked them in the eye. Places where their names weren't followed by red stamps or numbers or quiet whispers behind clipboards.

Annora was behind bars now.

Her empire of lies had fallen like a house of rotting cards. The files Mara had taken turned into headlines. The photos into fury. The truth into something so undeniable that not even money could muffle it.

She had tried to smile in the courtroom, the way she always had.

But no one smiled back.

And Mara?

Mara stood under a tree that had started blooming again.

The grave was small, neat. The name carved gently into the stone.

Leah Jane R.

You were loved. You are loved. Always.

A soft breeze carried the scent of wildflowers across the clearing. Mara knelt, fingers trembling as she tied a thin, delicate crown of daisies and baby's breath together—just like Leah used to make when they were kids, when the world felt safer under their shared sky.

She placed it on the top of the stone, careful, reverent.

"I brought Jane Eyre," she whispered, holding up the worn book. "Your favorite. I marked the page you loved most. The one where she says, *'I am no bird; and no net ensnares me.'* You always said it made you feel brave."

Her voice cracked, but she kept reading.

Each word wrapped around the silence like a balm. Not because Leah was gone—but because somehow, she wasn't.

A soft giggle drifted on the wind.

Mara froze.

She turned her head slowly—and there, by the far edge of the clearing, stood a girl.

Barefoot. Pale. Wide-eyed. A white ribbon in her hair.

Lana.

Her ghost shimmered faintly, like sunlight reflecting on water. She didn't speak—not with words—but her eyes said everything.

She pointed to the grave beside her.

Then she smiled.

"She's safe," Mara whispered, tears slipping free. "You're watching over her."

Lana nodded once.

And then she was gone.

But Mara didn't feel alone.

Not anymore.

Because grief had hollowed her—but love had filled those cracks with gold. Leah might not have made it out of that place, but she had made it *through* Mara. Through her courage. Through her fight. Through the world she had saved in Leah's name.

She would never stop missing her.

But for the first time in a long, long time...

She could breathe again.

And somewhere, in that place between then and now, spring and sorrow, childhood and goodbye—

Leah was laughing in a field of flowers. And Lana was braiding her a crown.

Author's Note

Thank you—truly—to everyone who read this story. I hope you give it the same love I poured into it, because every one of you matters so much to me. Knowing that you're reading my words, living in this world I created... it overwhelms me in the best way possible.

Writing *Daughters of Discipline* took me on a wild rollercoaster of emotions—rage, grief, hope, fire—and every word holds a piece of my heart. This book means the world to me, and so do your reviews, your thoughts, and your support.

If this story stayed with you, I hope you'll pass it on to someone who might need it too.

Lots of love always,
Maryam